The Tale of Dickie Deer Mouse

Arthur Scott Bailey

THE TALE OF DICKIE DEER MOUSE

I

A LITTLE GENTLEMAN

All the four-footed folk in the neighborhood agreed that Dickie Deer Mouse was well worth knowing. Throughout Pleasant Valley there was no one else so gentle as he.

To be sure, Jasper Jay wore beautiful—perhaps even gaudy—clothes; but his manners were so shocking that nobody would ever call him a gentleman.

As for Dickie Deer Mouse, he was always tastefully dressed in fawn color and white. And except sometimes in the spring, when he needed a new coat, he was a real joy to see. For he both looked and acted like a well-bred little person.

It is too bad that there were certain reasons—which will appear later—why some of his feathered neighbors did not like him. But even they had to admit that Dickie was a spick-and-span young chap.

Wherever he was white he was white as snow. And many of the wild people wondered how he could scamper so fast through the woods and always keep his white feet spotless.

Possibly it was because his mother had taught him the way when he was young; for his feet—and the under side of him—were white even when he was just a tiny fellow, so young that the top side of him was gray instead of fawn colored.

How his small white feet would twinkle as he frisked about in the shadows of the woods and ran like a squirrel through the trees! And how his sharp little cries would break the wood-silence as he called to his friends in a brisk chatter, which sounded like that of the squirrels, only ever so far away!

In many other ways Dickie Deer Mouse was like Frisky Squirrel himself. Dickie's idea of what a good home ought to be was much the same as Frisky's: they both thought that the deserted nest of one of the big Crow family made as fine a house as any one could want. And they couldn't imagine that any food could possibly be better than nuts, berries and grain.

To be sure, Dickie Deer Mouse liked his nuts to have thin shells. But that was because he was smaller than Frisky; so of course his jaws and teeth were not so strong.

Then, too, Dickie Deer Mouse had a trick of gathering good things to eat, which he hid away in some safe place, so that he would not have to go hungry during the winter, when the snow lay deep upon the ground. And even Frisky Squirrel was no spryer at carrying beechnuts—or any other goody—to his secret cupboard than little white-footed Dickie Deer Mouse.

It was no wonder that Dickie could be cheerful right in the dead of winter, when he had a fine store of the very best that the fields and forest yielded, to keep him sleek and fat and happy. So even on the coldest nights, when the icy wind whipped the tree-tops, and the cold, pale stars peeped down among the branches, Dickie scampered through the woods with his friends and had the gayest of times.

No one would have thought that he had a care in the world.

HUNTING A HOME

Warm weather was at hand. And Dickie Deer Mouse gave up frolicking with his friends for a time, because he needed to find a pleasant place in which to spend the summer.

He had his eye on a nest high in the top of a tall elm, where a certain black rascal known as old Mr. Crow had lived for a long while.

Now, Dickie had heard a bit of gossip, to the effect that the old gentleman had moved to another tree nearer to Farmer Green's cornfield. So Dickie wanted to lose no time. He was afraid that if he waited, some brisk member of the Squirrel family would settle himself in Mr. Crow's old home.

Without telling anybody what was in his head, Dickie Deer Mouse set forth one pleasant, warm night in the direction of the great elm, where he hoped to pass a number of delightful months.

It was some distance to the tall tree. But the night was fine, and Dickie enjoyed his journey, though once he stopped and shivered when he heard the wailing whistle of a screech owl.

"That's Simon Screecher!" Dickie Deer Mouse exclaimed under his breath. "I know his voice. And I hope he won't come this way!"

Dickie halted for a few minutes, near an old oak with spreading roots, under which he intended to hide in case Simon Screecher should suddenly appear.

But he soon decided that Simon was headed for another part of the woods, for his quavering cry grew fainter and fainter. So Dickie promptly forgot his fright and scampered on again faster than before, to make up the time he had lost.

Though he travelled through the flickering shadows like a brown and white streak, he did not pant the least bit when he reached old Mr. Crow's elm. He did not need to pause at the foot of the tree to get his breath, but scurried up it as if climbing was one of the easiest things he did.

Mr. Crow's big nest was so far from the ground that many people would not have cared to visit it except with the help of an elevator. But Dickie Deer Mouse never stopped to think of such a thing. Of course it would have done him no good, anyway, to wish for an elevator, for there was none in all Pleasant Valley. In fact, even Johnnie Green himself had only heard of—and never seen—one.

It took Dickie Deer Mouse only a few moments to reach the top of the tall elm, where Mr. Crow's bulky nest, built of sticks and lined with grass and moss, rested in a crotch formed by three branches.

Dickie had never before been so close to Mr. Crow's old home. And now he stood still and looked at it with great interest. It was ever so much bigger than he had supposed, and exactly the sort of dwelling—cool and airy— that he had hoped to find for his summer home.

"I don't see what sort of house the old gentleman can want that would be better than this," Dickie Deer Mouse remarked to himself. "But it is a long way from the cornfield, to be sure." And then he climbed quickly up the side of the nest and whisked down inside it.

The next moment a great commotion frightened him nearly out of his wits. A deafening squawking smote Dickie Deer Mouse's big ears. And something struck him a number of blows that knocked his breath quite out of him.

III

A STARTLED SLEEPER

Of course Dickie Deer Mouse ought not to have been so ready to believe that stray bit of gossip about Mr. Crow. It is true that the old black scamp had talked about moving to a new place nearer Farmer Green's cornfield. But his plan had gone no further than that.

He was sound asleep in his bed when Dickie Deer Mouse jumped down beside him. And when Mr. Crow suddenly waked up it would be very hard to say which of the two was the more startled.

For a few moments Mr. Crow screamed loudly for help. And he flapped and floundered about as if he didn't know which way to turn, nor what to do.

During the uproar Dickie Deer Mouse managed to slip out of Mr. Crow's house without being seen. But he was too polite to run away. Instead of hurrying off to escape a scolding from Mr. Crow he clung to a near-by branch and called as loudly as he could:

"Don't be alarmed, sir! There's no one here but me. And I ask your pardon for disturbing you."

Dickie Deer Mouse had to repeat that speech several times before Mr. Crow noticed him. But at last the old gentleman caught sight of his visitor. And when he heard what Dickie said he looked far from pleasant.

"Asking my pardon is one thing," Mr. Crow spluttered. "And receiving it is another."

"I'm very sorry," Dickie Deer Mouse replied. "I didn't mean to frighten you."

Mr. Crow gave a sudden hoarse haw-haw.

"Pooh!" he cried. "You don't think I was scared, do you?"

"You called for help," Dickie reminded him.

6

"Certainly I did," Mr. Crow agreed. "I wanted somebody to help you out of my house, before I trampled on you and broke one of your legs — or maybe two or three of 'em."

That explanation gave Dickie Deer Mouse another surprise; for he had supposed all the time that Mr. Crow didn't know who — or what — had awakened him.

"Oh!" he cried. "I thought that you thought I was somebody else."

Mr. Crow glared at him.

"I thought that you thought that I thought— —" he squalled. He was so angry that his tongue became sadly twisted; and he all but choked.

Meanwhile Dickie Deer Mouse waited respectfully until Mr. Crow had recovered his speech.

"What are you doing here at this hour?" Mr. Crow demanded at last.

"I thought— —" Dickie began.

"There you go again!" the old gentleman interrupted him testily. "I didn't ask you what you thought. I asked you what you were doing."

"I'm not doing anything just now," Dickie Deer Mouse faltered.

"Yes, you are!" Mr. Crow corrected him. "You're sitting on a limb of my tree.... Get off it at once!"

So Dickie Deer Mouse moved to a more distant perch.

"Now you're sitting on another!" Mr. Crow exploded. "Get out of my tree this instant!" It always made him ill-tempered to be awakened from a sound sleep in the middle of the night.

Once more Dickie Deer Mouse asked his pardon.

"I was told," he explained, "that you had moved lately. And I did not expect to find you here."

"Ah!" said Mr. Crow. "I know now why you came sneaking into my house. You'd like to live here yourself."

"Pardon me!" Dickie Deer Mouse exclaimed with the lowest of bows. "You are mistaken, Mr. Crow. Though your house is a fine, large one, it's much too small to hold us both."

And whisking about, while Mr. Crow stared at him, he ran down the tall elm as fast as he could go.

It was clear that if Mr. Crow wasn't going to move he would have to look elsewhere for a summer home.

IV

THE BLACKBIRD'S NEST

For a few days after his visit to Mr. Crow's elm, Dickie Deer Mouse kept watch carefully of Mr. Crow's comings and goings. And he decided at last that the old gentleman liked his home too well to leave it.

But Dickie was not discouraged. He had no doubt that he could find some other pleasant quarters in which to spend the summer—quarters that would prove almost as airy, and perhaps more convenient—because they were not so high.

For there was no denying that Mr. Crow's nest was a long, long way from the ground.

So Dickie began to search for birds' nests. And for a time he had to suffer a great deal of scolding by his feathered neighbors. It must be confessed that they were none too fond of Dickie Deer Mouse. There was a story of something he was said to have done one time—a tale about his having driven a Robin family away from their nest, in order to live in it himself.

That seems a strange deed on the part of anyone so gentle as Dickie Deer Mouse. But old Mr. Crow always declared that it was true. And Solomon Owl often remarked that he wished Dickie Deer Mouse would try to drive him away from his home in the hollow hemlock.

But during his hunt for birds' nests Dickie Deer Mouse was careful to keep away from Solomon Owl, and his cousin Simon Screecher, and all the rest of the Owl family. He contented himself with hasty peeps into nests built by such smaller folk as Blackbirds and Robins. And if it happened that anybody was living in one of those nests, Dickie soon found it out. For the angry owners were sure to fly at him with screams of rage, and peck at his head as they darted past him.

It was really not worth while getting into a fight over a bird's nest, when there was plenty of old ones in which nobody dwelt. To be sure, many of them were almost ready to fall apart. But Dickie Deer Mouse finally found one to his liking—a last year's bird's nest where two Blackbirds had reared a promising family. They had not come back to Pleasant Valley. And there was their house, almost as good as new, just waiting for some one to move in and make himself at home.

Nobody objected when Dickie took the old nest for his home, though many a bird in the neighborhood remarked in his hearing that he would hate to be too lazy to build a house for himself.

Dickie Deer Mouse was too mild and gentle-mannered to make any reply to such rude speeches. Besides, he expected to make a good many changes in the old nest before the place was exactly what he wanted.

"I don't understand," he said aloud to nobody in particular, "why most birds don't know how a house should be built. Of all the birds in Pleasant Valley the only good nest-builder I know is Long Bill Wren. He must be a very sensible fellow, because he puts a roof on his house."

Now, Dickie Deer Mouse may—or may not—have known that some of his bird neighbors were near at hand, watching him. Certainly they must have heard what he said, for they began to scold at the top of their voices. And one rude listener named Jasper Jay screamed with fine scorn:

"What do you know about building a nest?" And then he laughed harshly.

But Dickie Deer Mouse only looked very wise and said nothing.

V

DICKIE'S SUMMER HOME

Dickie Deer Mouse was busier than ever. When he wasn't looking for food—and eating it when he had found it—he gathered cat-tail down in Cedar Swamp.

If there was one thing that he liked in a house it was a soft bed. And he knew that if the weather happened to be chilly now and then, he could snuggle into the cat-tail down and sleep as comfortably as he pleased.

The swamp was none too near his new home; and he might have found moss or shreds of bark near-by that would have served his purpose. But he would rather have cat-tail down, even though he had to make a good many trips back and forth before he finally lined the old bird's nest to his liking.

Then, having finished his bed, he had to make a roof over it. So he covered the top of his house with moss, leaving a hole right under the eaves, for a doorway.

When Dickie's home was done he was so pleased with it that he asked all his neighbors if they didn't like his "improvements," as he called the additions he had made. And all his Deer Mouse relations told him that he certainly had a fine place.

But none of the birds cared for it at all, except Long Bill Wren; and even he remarked that the house would be better "if it was rounder."

As for Jasper Jay, he told Dickie Deer Mouse that, in his opinion, the house was ruined.

"It's nothing but a trap," he declared. "And I'd hate to go to sleep inside it."

His views, however, did not trouble Dickie Deer Mouse in the least. The place suited him. And he was so happy in it that sometimes when the weather was bad and he wasn't whisking about in the trees, or scurrying around on the ground, he would stay inside his cozy home, with only his

11

head sticking out through the doorway, while his big, bright, bulging, black eyes took in everything that happened in his dooryard.

Dickie Deer Mouse knew that one needed sharp eyes to spy him when he was peeping from his house in that fashion. And often when somebody of whom he was really afraid came wandering through the woods, Dickie would keep quite still, while he watched the newcomer without being seen.

But with some of the wood folk he took no chances. Whenever he heard Solomon Owl's rolling call, or his cousin Simon Screecher's quavering whistle, Dickie Deer Mouse always pulled his head inside his house in a hurry.

For they were usually on the lookout for him. And he knew it.

Of course, if they had been aware that Dickie Deer Mouse was hidden inside his rebuilt, last year's bird's nest, either of them, with his sharp claws, could easily have torn the moss roof off Dickie's home. But luckily for Dickie, there were some things that they didn't know.

VI

A WARNING

If old Mr. Crow had minded his own affairs everything would have gone well with Dickie Deer Mouse, after he moved into his new home. But Mr. Crow could not forget the time when Dickie had awakened him out of a sound sleep and frightened him almost out of his mind.

So whenever he caught sight of Dickie the old gentleman was sure to drop down upon the ground and ask him in a loud voice whose house he had prowled into lately.

"Nobody's!" Dickie Deer Mouse always told him. And then he would assure Mr. Crow that he was very sorry to have disturbed his rest.

It was quite like Mr. Crow, on such occasions, to act grumpy.

"I haven't had a good night's sleep since you broke into my house," he declared to Dickie one day.

"Perhaps you're over-eating," Dickie suggested politely.

Old Mr. Crow did not appear to like that remark.

"Nothing of the sort!" he bawled. "I don't eat enough to keep a mosquito alive."

"I often see you in the cornfield," Dickie Deer Mouse told him.

"Ha!" Mr. Crow exclaimed. "What are you doing in the cornfield, I should like to know?"

"Sometimes I go there to get a few kernels of corn," Dickie explained.

"Ha!" Mr. Crow cried once more. "That's where the corn's going! Farmer Green thinks I'm taking it. And so you're getting me into a peck of trouble, young man."

Dickie Deer Mouse couldn't help being worried when Mr. Crow said that. And he looked puzzled, too.

"I don't see," he said, "how I could have got you into a peck of trouble, Mr. Crow, for I haven't eaten a peck of Farmer Green's corn. I've had only a few kernels of it—not more than half a pint."

"Then you've got me into a half-pint of trouble, anyway," old Mr. Crow insisted. "And that's too much, for a person of my age. You'll have to keep away from my—ahem!—from Farmer Green's cornfield. And what's more, Fatty Coon says the same thing."

At the mention of Fatty Coon's name Dickie Deer Mouse had to smile.

"Fatty Coon!" he echoed. "How he does like corn!"

"Yes! But he doesn't like you," Mr. Crow snapped. "You'd better look out for him," he warned Dickie. "He'll come to call on you some night, the first thing you know.

"By the way, where are you living now?" Mr. Crow inquired.

But Dickie Deer Mouse made no answer. Right before Mr. Crow's sharp eyes he vanished among the roots of a tree. And it made the old gentleman quite peevish because he couldn't discover where Dickie Deer Mouse had hidden himself.

For a little while Mr. Crow stood like a black statue and peered at the tangle where Dickie Deer Mouse had disappeared. But Mr. Crow couldn't see him anywhere. And at last his patience came to an end.

"He never answered my question," Mr. Crow grumbled. "He wouldn't tell me where he lived. But I'll find out. I'll ask my cousin, Jasper Jay; for there isn't much that he doesn't know."

VII

NOISY VISITORS

Of course Jasper Jay knew where Dickie Deer Mouse lived. And he took great pleasure in pointing out the exact spot to his curious cousin, old Mr. Crow.

It was broad daylight when they visited the tree where Dickie's house hung. The two rogues did not know that he was drowsing inside his snug home, because he had been out late the night before.

No one that knew the two cousins would need to be told that they could never talk together quietly. Perched close to Dickie's house, Mr. Crowcroaked in a hoarse voice, while Jasper Jay squalled harshly.

"This is it!" Jasper had announced, as soon as they arrived. "This is his house. And isn't it a sight?"

"I should say so!" old Mr. Crow agreed. "It's got a roof on it—ha! ha!"

And the two visitors laughed loudly, as if they thought there was a huge joke somewhere.

They made such a noise, from the very first, that Dickie Deer Mouse awoke and heard almost everything they said. But he didn't mind their remarks in the least—until he caught Fatty Coon's name.

It was old Mr. Crow who mentioned it first.

"I'll have to tell Fatty Coon about this queer house," he chuckled. "It's too good a joke to keep. He'll be over here as soon as he knows where to come, for he'll be glad to see it; and he wants to talk to Dickie Deer Mouse about taking our corn."

Dickie had still felt somewhat sleepy during the first part of this talk outside his house. But when Mr. Crow began to speak about Fatty Coon, Dickie became instantly wide awake. He sprang quickly to his feet; and thrusting his head through his doorway, he called in his loudest tone:

"When do you think Fatty Coon will call on me?"

The two cousins looked at each other. And then they looked all around.

"What was that strange squeaking?" Mr. Crow asked Jasper Jay.

"To me it sounded a good deal like a rusty hinge on Farmer Green's barn door," Jasper Jay answered.

But Mr. Crow shook his head. "It couldn't have been that," he said.

"Maybe Mrs. Green is rocking on a loose board on the porch," Jasper suggested.

Still Mr. Crow couldn't agree with him.

"Don't be silly!" he snapped. "We're half a mile from the farmhouse."

"Well, what do you think the noise was?" Jasper Jay inquired.

Old Mr. Crow cocked an eye upward into the tree-top above him. "I'd think it was a Squirrel if it was louder," he replied. Jasper Jay laughed in a most disagreeable fashion.

"I'd think it was thunder if it was loud enough," he sneered.

And at that the two cousins began to quarrel violently. To tell the truth, they never could be together long without having a dispute.

For a short time Dickie Deer Mouse listened to their rude remarks, hoping that they would stop wrangling long enough to hear his question about Fatty Coon.

But they talked louder and louder. And since Dickie Deer Mouse never quarreled with anybody, and hated to hear such language as the two cousins used, he slipped out of his house without their seeing him and went over to the cornfield.

For he was hungry.

VIII

IN THE CORNFIELD

In one way, especially, Fatty Coon and Dickie Deer Mouse were alike: They were night-prowlers. When they slept it was usually broad daylight outside, and the birds—except for a few odd fellows like Willie Whip-poor-will and Mr. Night Hawk—were abroad, and singing, and twittering. And when most of the birds went to sleep Dickie and Fatty Coon began to feel quite wide awake.

It was not strange, therefore, that Dickie Deer Mouse was surprised when he found himself face to face with Fatty Coon in the cornfield at midday.

Dickie tried to slip out of sight under a pumpkin vine that grew between the rows; but Fatty Coon saw him before he could hide. And Fatty began to make the queerest noise, as if he were almost choking.

Dickie Deer Mouse stopped. And he trembled the least bit; for Fatty looked terribly fierce. Perhaps (Dickie thought) he was choking with rage.

"Can I help you?" Dickie asked him. "Would you like me to thump you on the back?"

Fatty Coon shook his head. There was nothing the matter with him, except that he had stuffed his mouth so full that he couldn't speak. After swallowing several times he wiped his mouth on the back of his paw—a habit of which his mother had never been able to break him. It was no wonder that dainty Dickie Deer Mouse shuddered again, when Fatty did that.

"May I go and get you a napkin?" Dickie asked, as he edged away.

"No!" Fatty Coon growled. "I've been wanting to have a talk with you. And now that I've found you, you needn't run off."

Then, to Dickie's horror, Fatty stopped talking and licked both his paws.

"May I get you a finger bowl?" Dickie inquired.

Fatty Coon actually didn't know what he meant.

"Is that something to eat?" he asked. And he looked much interested, and seemed quite downcast when Dickie said "No!"

"Then you needn't trouble yourself," Fatty Coon told him with a sigh.

"Can't you find corn enough for a good meal?" Dickie asked him wonderingly.

"I could," said Fatty Coon, "if other people didn't take so much of it.... Now, there's Mr. Crow," he complained. "I had to get out of bed and come over here to-day, in the sunlight, because I was afraid he wouldn't leave any corn for me.

"There's no use saying anything to him," Fatty continued, "because he thinks this is his cornfield.... But little chaps like you will have to keep away from this place.... Now I've warned you," he added. "And if I hear of your eating any more corn I'll come straight to your house—when I find out where it is—and I'll — — "

He did not finish his threat. But he looked so darkly at Dickie that what he didn't say made Dickie Deer Mouse shiver all over, though the warm midday sun fell upon the cornfield.

Now, Dickie Deer Mouse hadn't eaten a single kernel of corn all that day. But he suddenly lost his appetite for it; and murmuring a faint good-bye he turned and ran for the woods as fast as he could go.

"Stop! Stop!" Fatty Coon called after him. "There's something more I want to say to you."

But whatever it may have been, Dickie Deer Mouse did not wait to hear it.

IX

FATTY COON NEEDS HELP

THE moment he plunged into the woods beyond the cornfield Dickie Deer Mouse began to feel better. He knew that Fatty Coon would not leave that place of plenty until he had filled himself almost to bursting with tender young corn.

After Dickie had eaten a few seeds that he found under the trees, as well as a plump bug that was hiding beneath a log, he actually told himself that he was glad he had met Fatty Coon in the cornfield.

"Now that he has talked with me," Dickie reasoned, "he won't trouble himself to come to my house when old Mr. Crow tells him where I live."

That thought was a great comfort to him. Ever since he had waked up and heard Mr. Crow and Jasper Jay talking outside his house he had felt most uneasy. If Mr. Crow was going to guide Fatty Coon to his new home, Dickie hardly thought it safe to stay there any longer.

But now he was sure that that danger was past. Fatty had given him his warning. And Dickie had no doubt that so long as he kept away from the corn his greedy neighbor would never bother to disturb him.

So instead of quitting his snug home — as he had feared he must — he went back to it to finish his nap.

Now, Dickie Deer Mouse had lost so much sleep — through being disturbed by Mr. Crow and Jasper Jay — that when night came he kept right on sleeping. Yes! Instead of joining his friends in a mad scamper through the woods in the moonlight, Dickie Deer Mouse slept on and on and on, until — something shook the small tree where he lived and made it sway as if an earthquake had come.

Dickie Deer Mouse roused himself with a start. His sharp ears caught a scratching sound. And sticking his head through his doorway, he looked out.

One quick glance told him what was happening. That pudgy rascal, Fatty Coon, was climbing the tree! And every moment brought him nearer and nearer to Dickie's house.

Dickie's big, black eyes bulged more than ever as he whisked out of his house and scampered to the top of the tree, where the branches were so small that Fatty Coon could never follow him.

"Stop!" Fatty Coon cried. "Mr. Crow told me where I could find you. And I want to have a word with you."

"What sort of word?" Dickie Deer Mouse inquired.

"It's about the cornfield," Fatty Coon explained.

"I haven't been near that place since you last saw me there," Dickie declared.

"I know you haven't," Fatty told him. "That's just why I want to have a word with you. I'm in a peck of trouble. And I want you to help me."

Dickie Deer Mouse could scarcely believe it. But being a very polite young gentleman, he told Fatty that he would be glad to do anything in his power to assist him — or at least, anything except to come down out of the top of the tree.

X

A BIT OF ADVICE

"IT'S like this," Fatty Coon said, puffing a bit—on account of his climb—as he looked up at Dickie Deer Mouse. "Old Mr. Crow says that Farmer Green is going to sick old dog Spot on me if I don't keep out of the cornfield."

"Well, I should say it was very kind of Mr. Crow to tell you," Dickie remarked.

Fatty Coon was not so sure of that.

"He'd like to have the cornfield to himself," he told Dickie. "He'd like nothing better than to keep me out of it. And if old dog Spot is coming there after me, I certainly don't want to go near the place again."

"Then I'd stay away, if I were you," Dickie Deer Mouse told him.

"Ah! That's just the trouble!" Fatty Coon cried. "I can't! I'm too fond of corn. And that's why I've come here to have a word with you," he went on. "I've noticed that you haven't set foot in the cornfield since I spoke to you over there in the middle of the day. And I want you to tell me how you manage to stay away."

"Something seems to pull me right away from it," Dickie Deer Mouse told him.

Fatty Coon groaned.

"Something seems to pull me towards the corn!" he wailed.

Dickie Deer Mouse couldn't help feeling sorry for him.

"If there was only something else that you liked better than green corn," he said, "perhaps it would help you to keep away from this new danger."

"But there isn't!" Fatty Coon exclaimed.

"Have you ever tried horns?" Dickie Deer Mouse asked him.

Fatty Coon looked puzzled.

"What kind?" he asked his small friend.

"Deer's!" Dickie explained. "You know they drop them in the woods sometimes. I've had many a meal off deer's horns. And I can say truthfully that there's nothing quite like them when you're hungry."

Fatty Coon actually began to look hopeful.

"I'm always hungry," he announced. "And perhaps if I could get a taste of deer's horns they would keep my mind off the cornfield. Where did you say I could find some?"

"I didn't say," Dickie Deer Mouse reminded him; "but I don't object to telling you where to look. They're generally to be found in the woods, near the foot of a tree."

Fatty Coon's face brightened at once.

"Then it ought to be easy for me to get a taste of some," he cried. And he began to crawl down the tree even as he spoke.

He did not thank Dickie Deer Mouse for his help. But that was like Fatty. Always having his mind on eatables, he was more than likely to forget to be polite.

Little Dickie Deer Mouse smiled as he watched the actions of his late caller. The instant Fatty Coon reached the ground he began to look under the trees — first one and then another.

"Don't miss a single tree!" Dickie called to him.

"Don't worry!" Fatty Coon replied. "I'm going to keep looking until I find some deer's horns. And I hope I'll like 'em when I find 'em, for I'm terribly hungry right now."

A SEARCH IN VAIN

IT was true that Dickie Deer Mouse and all his relations feasted on the horns shed by the deer. But of course they didn't find horns in the woods every day. Only at a certain season of the year did the deer drop them. And since that time was now past, and the Deer Mouse family had scoured the woods until they found — and devoured — them all, it is clear that Fatty Coon had started out on a fruitless hunt.

But he didn't know that, even if Dickie Deer Mouse did. And that was the reason why Dickie smiled as he watched Fatty Coon dodging about among the trees, looking for deer's horns where there couldn't possibly be any.

"It's the finest thing that could happen to Fatty," Dickie Deer Mouse thought. "While he's hunting for horns he can't go to the cornfield. And so long as he stays away from the cornfield, old dog Spot can't catch him there."

And then Dickie set forth to find his friends and enjoy a romp in the moonlight.

Dawn found him creeping into his house once more. And after what had happened during the night it was not strange that he should dream about Fatty Coon.

It was not a pleasant dream. For some reason or other Fatty Coon seemed to be angry with him, and was shouting in a terrible, deep voice, "Where's Dickie Deer Mouse? Where's Dickie Deer Mouse?"

And then Dickie awoke, all a-shiver. But of course he felt better at once, for he knew that it was only a dream. And he stretched himself, and buried his head in his bed of cat-tail down, because the daylight was trickling in through his doorway.

"Where's Dickie Deer Mouse?" Again that question startled him, though he was wide awake, and couldn't be dreaming.

The next instant Dickie's tree began to quiver. Fatty Coon was climbing up it! And Dickie Deer Mouse jumped out of bed in a hurry and slipped out of his door.

Looking down, he could see that Fatty Coon was in something quite like a rage.

"What's the matter?" Dickie called to him.

Fatty could do nothing but glare and growl at him.

"Have you had your breakfast?" Dickie asked him.

Fatty shook his head.

"No!" he roared. "I haven't had a morsel to eat since I last saw you. I've been hunting for horns all this time. And I've come back to tell you that I don't like your advice. If I followed it much longer there's no doubt that I'd starve to death."

"It has kept you out of the cornfield, hasn't it?" Dickie inquired.

"Yes!" Fatty admitted. "But it won't much longer. I'm on my way to the cornfield now." He looked at Dickie and frowned, as if to say, "Just try to stop me!"

"Aren't you afraid to go there?" Dickie asked him.

Fatty Coon sniffed.

"That story about old dog Spot was nothing but a trick," he declared. "It was just a trick of old Mr. Crow's. He wants all the corn himself."

"Don't you think, then, that you and I ought to eat all the corn we can?" Dickie inquired.

"I certainly do!" Fatty Coon replied. "Let's hurry over now and get some!"

Dickie Deer Mouse was only too glad to accept the invitation. And he waited politely until Fatty had reached the ground, before going down himself.

Old Mr. Crow saw them the moment they entered the cornfield. And he hurried up to them with a most important air and advised them both that they "had come to a dangerous place."

Fatty Coon paid no attention to the old gentleman.

But Dickie Deer Mouse thanked Mr. Crow and told him that after he had had all the corn he wanted he was going back to the woods.

Noticing that the old gentleman seemed peevish about something, Dickie said to him:

"There ought to be enough for all."

But still Mr. Crow looked glum.

"There's enough for them that don't care for much else," he muttered. "But we can't feed the whole world on this corn, you know.... How would you like it if I took to eating deer's horns — when they're in season, of course?"

"You can have all the deer's horns you want," Fatty Coon remarked thickly — for already his mouth was full.

And being very polite, Dickie Deer Mouse said the same thing; though of course he waited until he could speak distinctly.

XII

A LITTLE SURPRISE

SIMON SCREECHER lived in the apple orchard, in a hollow tree, where he could sleep during the day safe from attack by mobs of small birds, who had the best of reasons for disliking him.

By night Simon wandered about the fields and the woods, hunting for mice and insects. And since night was the time when Dickie Deer Mouse was awake, and up and doing, it would have been a wonder if the two had never met.

One thing is certain: Dickie Deer Mouse was not eager to make Simon Screecher's acquaintance. Whenever he heard Simon's call he stopped and listened. If it sounded nearer the next time it reached his ears, Dickie Deer Mouse promptly hid himself in any good place that was handy.

So matters went along for some time. And Dickie actually began to think that perhaps he didn't need to be so careful, and that maybe Simon Screecher was not so bad as people said.

However, he jumped almost out of his skin one night, when he heard a wailing whistle in a tree right over his head. And when he came down upon all-fours again he couldn't see a single place to hide.

So he stood stock still, hardly daring to breathe.

To Dickie's dismay, a mocking laugh rang out. And somebody said:

"I see you!"

It was Simon Screecher himself that spoke.

Dickie Deer Mouse looked up and spied him, sitting on a low limb. He was not so big as Dickie had supposed. But it was certainly Simon. Dickie knew him, beyond a doubt, by his ear-tufts, which stuck up from his head like horns.

"What made you jump when I whistled?" Simon Screecher asked him.

"I don't know," Dickie answered, "unless it was you."

Simon Screecher chuckled.

"You're a bright young chap," he observed. "But that's not surprising, for I notice that you belong to the Deer Mouse family, and everybody's aware that they are one of the brightest families in Pleasant Valley — what are left of them."

These last words made Dickie Deer Mouse more uneasy than ever. But he made up his mind not to let Simon Screecher know that he was worried.

"I have a great many relations," he declared stoutly. "Ours is a big family."

"Yes — but not nearly so big as it was when I first came to this neighborhood to live," Simon told him with a sly smile.

He had hardly finished that remark when a loud wha-wha, whoo-ah came from a hemlock not far away. And the next moment Simon's cousin Solomon Owl sailed through the moonlight and alighted near him.

Dickie Deer Mouse couldn't help thinking that it was a great night for the Owl family. And he was surprised to notice that Simon Screecher did not act overjoyed at seeing his cousin.

"It's a pleasant night," said Solomon Owl in his deep, hollow voice.

Simon Screecher replied somewhat sourly that he supposed it was. And he changed his seat, so that he might keep his eyes on both his cousin and Dickie Deer Mouse at the same time.

But Solomon Owl made matters very hard for Simon. Simon had no sooner seated himself comfortably when Solomon Owl moved to a perch behind him.

Simon Screecher looked almost crosseyed, as he tried to watch everything that happened. And he looked so fretful that for a moment Dickie Deer Mouse actually forgot his fear and laughed aloud.

XIII

THE FEATHERS FLY

"I'M glad to see you," Solomon Owl told his cousin Simon Screecher, while Dickie Deer Mouse stood stock still on the ground beneath the tree where the two cousins were sitting. "I'm glad to see you. And I hope you're enjoying good health."

"I'm well enough," Simon Screecher grunted.

"Do you find plenty to eat nowadays?" Solomon asked him.

Simon Screecher admitted that he was not starving.

"Ah!" Solomon exclaimed. "Then you can have no objection to sharing a specially nice tidbit with your own cousin."

Dickie Deer Mouse shivered. But he did not dare move, with one of Simon Screecher's great, glassy eyes staring straight at him. And there was something else that did not help to put him at his ease: Solomon Owl seemed to be watching him likewise!

"Haven't you dined to-night?" Simon Screecher inquired in a testy tone.

"Yes!" Solomon admitted. "But I haven't had my dessert yet.... What are you looking at so closely, Cousin Simon, down there on the ground?"

An angry light came into Simon Screecher's eyes.

"Can't I look where I please?" he snapped.

And he changed his seat again, so that he might get a better view of Dickie and Solomon at the same time.

Solomon Owl promptly moved to another limb behind Simon, and slightly higher.

And Dickie Deer Mouse took heart when Simon Screecher began to make a queer sound by opening his beak and shutting it with a snap, as if he would like to nip somebody.

Dickie knew that Simon Screecher was in a terrible rage. And unless his threatening actions scared Solomon Owl away, Dickie thought there was likely to be a cousinly fight.

He was pleased to notice that Solomon Owl showed no sign of dismay. There was really no reason why he should. He was much bigger than his peppery cousin. And he looked at Simon in a calm and unruffled fashion that seemed to make that quarrelsome fellow angrier than ever.

"What's the matter?" Solomon Owl asked Simon Screecher. "If you had any teeth I'd think they were chattering.... Are you having a chill?"

Simon made no answer.

"Maybe you're afraid of something," Solomon Owl suggested. "Can it be that young Deer Mouse down there on the ground?" And he laughed loudly at what he thought was a joke.

"That's my Deer Mouse!" Simon Screecher squalled, suddenly finding his voice. "I saw him first. And he's my prize."

"He looks to me like the one I lost a few nights ago," Solomon Owl announced solemnly. "In that case, of course I saw him first. So you'd better fly home to your old apple tree in the orchard."

"I'll do nothing of the sort!" Simon Screecher declared; and his voice rose to a shrill quaver.

Turning swiftly, he flew straight at his cousin. And then how the feathers did fly!

Dickie Deer Mouse wanted to stay right there, for he hated to miss any of the fun. But he remembered that he was a "tidbit"; so he scampered away through the woods. And though he never knew how the fight ended, he was sure of one thing: There was no prize for the winner.

XIV

MAKING READY FOR WINTER

AFTER his escape from Solomon Owl and Simon Screecher, Dickie Deer Mouse never felt quite so care-free as he always had before, when wandering through the woods at night. And he never stayed inside his house after dark without wondering whether Solomon or Simon could by any chance discover his snug home in the last year's bird's nest. It was not a pleasant thought. And the oftener it popped into Dickie's head the less he liked it.

Sometimes, when summer had ended and fall brought a night that was rainy and cold, he liked to go home after he had finished his supper, and burrow deep into his soft bed of cat-tail down.

But even after he had dried his wet coat and warmed himself well, at such times Dickie Deer Mouse started whenever he heard the slightest noise. Somehow, he couldn't get the Owl family out of his mind.

As the days grew shorter — and the nights longer — he began to find that his summer home was not so cozy as it might have been.

The cold wind searched him out, even under his soft covering; and the driving rains trickled annoyingly through his roof of moss.

So at last Dickie Deer Mouse made up his mind that he would move once more. And since he was not the sort to put off the doing of anything that had to be done, he set out at once to see what kind of place he could find.

Now, Dickie Deer Mouse liked the woods in which he had always lived. So one might think it strange that when he set forth on his search he headed straight for Farmer Green's pasture. But there is no doubt that he knew what he was about.

For some time he crept cautiously about the pasture, peeping under big rocks, and moving among the roots of the trees which dotted the hillside here and there. And since his eyes were of the sharpest, what he was looking for he found in surprising numbers.

Most people, strolling through the pasture, would have noticed little except grass and bushes, trees and rocks and knolls. But those were not the things that Dickie Deer Mouse discovered, and sniffed at. What he was hunting for was holes.

For Dickie had decided that when winter came, with its ice and snow, its cruel gales and its piercing cold, he would be far more comfortable underground than he could ever hope to be in a last year's bird's nest that was fastened to a tree.

He had found it no easy matter to pick out a summer home. And now there were reasons why his search for a winter one was even harder.

It is true that at the beginning of summer, when Dickie Deer Mouse climbed the tall elm where Mr. Crow lived, he found the old gentleman asleep in the nest that he had hoped to take for his own. But on the whole it was easy to discover whether a nest was deserted.

One look into it usually told the story. Eggs in a bird's nest meant that somebody must live there. And of course if Dickie saw a bird sitting on a nest he knew right away that he couldn't live there without having a fight first.

But a hole is different. One can't see what's at the bottom of it without going inside it.

And that is not always a pleasant thing to do.

XV

A PLUNGE IN THE DARK

THERE was one hole, especially, among those he found in Farmer Green's pasture, from which Dickie Deer Mouse ran as fast as he could scamper.

This was a hole with a big front door, and plenty of fresh dirt scattered around it, as if somebody had been digging there not long before.

When Dickie first noticed the burrow he stopped short and stood quite still, while he peeped at it out of a tangle of blackberry bushes.

Something told him that he had stumbled upon the home of a dangerous person. And if the wind hadn't been blowing in his face, as he looked towards the wide opening, he would not have dared stay there as long as he did.

As he looked he suddenly saw a pair of eyes gleaming from the dark cavern. And soon he beheld a long, pointed snout, which its owner thrust outside in a gingerly manner.

That was enough for Dickie Deer Mouse.

He wheeled about and whisked up the nearest tree he could find. And there he stayed for a long, long time, until he felt sure that it was quite safe for him to venture down upon the ground again.

He had come upon Tommy Fox's burrow!

And if there was one hole in the ground into which he had no wish to go, that was it. For Tommy Fox was no friend of his.

Since he didn't care for Tommy's company, Dickie went to the corner of the pasture that was furthest from Tommy's home, to search once more for such a hole as he hoped to find.

Almost nobody else ever would have discovered the one that Dickie picked out at last as the best place of all in which to spend the winter. But the bright eyes of Dickie Deer Mouse found a tiny opening, which he carefully made just big enough to admit him.

It was the entrance to an old burrow where an aunt and an uncle of Billy Woodchuck had once lived and raised a numerous family. When the children had all grown up and gone away their parents had left that home for a new one in the clover field. And somehow all the smaller field people had overlooked it.

Little by little the frost had heaved the earth about the doorway, and the wash of the rains had helped to fill it, and Farmer Green's cows had trampled over it, and the grass had all but covered the small opening that remained.

There were signs in plenty about the spot that told Dickie Deer Mouse the burrow was deserted. Or perhaps it would be better to say that there was no sign at all of any occupant. Dickie found not a trace of a path nor even a foot-print near the hole nor did his nose discover the faintest scent either of friend or enemy.

Slipping inside the hole, Dickie found himself in the mouth of a big, airy tunnel, which went sharply downwards for a few feet.

And without the slightest fear he plunged down the dark hole, to see what he could see.

XVI

A LUCKY FIND

THOUGH Dickie Deer Mouse was shy, he couldn't have been a coward. For when he had reached the end of that first pitch that led into the old burrow of Billy Woodchuck's uncle and aunt he never once thought of turning back. Before him stretched a dark, dry, level tunnel. And through it Dickie quickly made his way.

It was surprisingly long—that underground passage. But he came to the end of it at last. And creeping upwards, because the tunnel rose suddenly, Dickie Deer Mouse found himself in a roomy chamber, comfortably furnished with a big bed of soft, dried grasses, where Mr. and Mrs. Woodchuck had passed a good many hard winters asleep, while the snow lay deep upon the ground above them.

It took Dickie Deer Mouse no longer than a jiffy to decide that he had found the very place for which he had been looking. He knew that in that secret chamber he had nothing to fear from Solomon Owl nor Simon Screecher, nor Fatty Coon, either. And when midwinter came, and the nights turned bitterly cold, he could cuddle down in that soft bed and dream about summer, and warm, moonlit nights in the woods of the world above.

It was no wonder that Dickie Deer Mouse was pleased. And for a time he forgot everything but his good luck—until he remembered that he had had nothing to eat since the night before.

So he made his way back through the long tunnel, and up into Farmer Green's pasture. Then, looking around under the twinkling stars, he took pains to see exactly where his new home was.

It certainly would have been a great mishap if he had gone away in such a hurry that he could never have found his doorway again. But it was an easy matter to fix the spot in his mind. When he came back he needed only to follow along the rail fence until he came to the corner. Not far from the fence corner, in the woods, stood Farmer Green's sugar house. And about the same distance on the other side of the fence a lone straggler of a maple tree stood on a knoll in the pasture. The departed Mr. and Mrs. Woodchuck had been wise enough to dig the opening to their burrow between the roots of the tree. They knew that if Tommy Fox tried to dig them out of their underground home, he would find the passage between the roots too small to squeeze through.

Dickie Deer Mouse smiled as he saw what the builders of his house had done. They had made everything exactly to suit him. He knew that he could have done no better himself; in fact he knew that he couldn't have done nearly so well. For he was no digger. But he told himself that there was no reason why he should feel sad about that, so long as others were kind enough to dig a fine home and leave it for him to live in.

Then he slipped into the woods, feeling so happy that he had to stop and relate his good fortune to the first person he met.

And that was where Dickie Deer Mouse made a slight mistake.

A SLIGHT MISTAKE

SCARCELY had Dickie Deer Mouse plunged into the woods when he met Fatty Coon coming in the opposite direction.

"Hullo!" Fatty said, looking up at Dickie, who had scrambled into a tree as soon as he caught sight of Fatty's plump form. "What have you been doing in Farmer Green's pasture! I thought you always stayed in the woods — unless you happened to go to the cornfield."

"I've been looking for a winter home," Dickie explained. "And I've just found the finest one you ever saw."

"Where is it!" Fatty asked him. "I might want to pay you a call some night — when I had nothing else to do."

Dickie Deer Mouse was in such a cheerful mood that almost anything Fatty Coon might have said would have pleased him.

"My new house is just beyond the fence," Dickie explained. "But I'm afraid you can't very well visit me there," he added with a smile.

"Why not?" Fatty Coon inquired. "I'm as good a climber as anybody. I can climb the tallest tree you ever saw, without feeling dizzy. But of course I'm a bit heavier than you are. And if you've gone and picked out a nest that's a long way above the ground, among the smallest branches, it might not be safe for me to go all the way up to it."

Dickie Deer Mouse had to smile once more.

"My new home isn't as high as I am right now," he told Fatty Coon.

Fatty grunted.

"Then I'll certainly come to see you," he said, "when time hangs heavily on my hands."

"My new house isn't as high as you are right now," Dickie remarked.

And at that Fatty Coon looked puzzled. His mouth fell open; and for a few moments he stared at his small friend without saying a word.

"You must be mistaken," he replied at last. "I'm standing on the ground. And I never saw a last year's bird's nest that was lower than that."

"I shall have to explain," said Dickie, "that my new home is much finer than my old one. Now, you may not believe it, but it has a front hall that's a hundred times as long as your tail."

Fatty Coon looked around at his ringed tail, with its black tip; and then he looked up at Dickie Deer Mouse again.

"You must be mistaken!" he cried. "I'll have to take my tail to your house and measure your front hall myself before I'll believe that."

"You can't measure my hall!" Dickie Deer Mouse exclaimed.

"Who's going to stop me?" Fatty Coon growled. He was used to having his own way. And it always made him angry when anybody tried to upset his plans. "I'm going to your house in the pasture now; and I'll soon show you that you're mistaken about your front hall.... You come with me and lead the way, young fellow!"

But Dickie Deer Mouse said he was so hungry that he couldn't go back just then.

"I'm headed for the big beech tree to see if I can find a few nuts," he announced.

At the mention of food Fatty Coon's face took on a different look.

"I'm hungry myself," he said, as if he had just remembered something. "I was on my way to Farmer Green's corn house when I met you. And I really ought to get there before the moon comes up. So if you'll tell me where your house is I'll stop there when I come back."

"My new home— —" Dickie Deer Mouse informed him with an air of great pride— —"my new home is in the burrow where Mr. and Mrs. Woodchuck used to live. The front door is under the tree that stands on the knoll just beyond the fence. But you can never get inside it, because you're altogether too fat."

The stout person on the ground knew that he spoke the truth. And without saying another word he turned about and disappeared in the direction of the farm buildings.

"Don't forget to take your tail with you!" Dickie Deer Mouse called to him, just before he was out of sight. "You might want to measure the corn house."

But Fatty Coon did not trouble himself to answer.

XVIII

TOO MANY COUSINS

IN high spirits Dickie Deer Mouse hurried on through the woods until he came to the big beech tree. And though many others had been there before him, since the nuts had ripened, Dickie had such a sharp eye for a beech nut that even though it was then night, he soon found enough for a hearty meal.

Then he had to have a romp with a few gay fellows whom he met under the beech tree. And so quickly did the time pass that before he knew it the night had turned gray. Day was breaking. And shouting good-bye to his friends Dickie Deer Mouse ran off towards Farmer Green's pasture. He wanted a nap. And having nothing in his summer home that was worth moving, he knew of no reason why he shouldn't begin at once to live in his new quarters.

He never felt happier than he did as he scampered in and out among the trees, slipped under the rail fence, and streaked across the short grass of the pasture. But when he reached his doorway he stopped in dismay.

Where he had expected to see nobody at all, his eyes bulged with surprise at the crowd that had gathered in his dooryard.

As soon as he had taken several good looks at the company, Dickie Deer Mouse discovered that they were distant relations of his, of all ages and sizes. And at last he succeeded in sorting them into families.

There were three big families. And no one in the whole crowd paid any heed to Dickie Deer Mouse. They seemed to be talking about something most important, and too busy to notice the newcomer.

If the truth were known, the sight of his second and third and fourth cousins did not particularly please Dickie Deer Mouse. But he was an agreeable young gentleman. So he stepped forward and called several of his cousins by name. And since he couldn't say honestly that he was delighted to see them, he told them how well they looked and said that he hoped they had passed a happy summer.

"Here he is at last!" everybody cried. "We've been waiting for you for a long time, because we weren't sure whether we'd found the right place."

"What place?" Dickie Deer Mouse asked them as he looked from one to another in dismay.

"Why, the great house that you've found!" somebody cried. "We've heard that it has a front hall a hundred times as long as Fatty Coon's tail. So of course there must be lots of rooms in it; and we've come to keep you company and spend the winter."

When he heard that news Dickie Deer Mouse became almost faint. He did not want to hurt his cousins' feelings. But his plan of spending the winter quietly hardly made him welcome the idea of having a dozen half-grown children in his home.

"Who told you about my house?" he demanded with just a trace of disappointment.

"It was Fatty Coon," several of his cousins explained at once.

And then Dickie Deer Mouse knew that he had made a mistake when he told Fatty of his good fortune.

"I'm sorry to say that he has misled you," Dickie informed his relations. "It's true that my front hall is very long. But the trouble is, there's only one chamber."

THE WRONG TURN

FOR a few moments Dickie Deer Mouse's cousins looked terribly disappointed. He had told them that his new house had only one chamber. And each of the three big families had expected to have at least one bedroom.

The elder cousins gathered in a group and talked in low tones. Dickie could not hear what they said. He hoped that they were going to bid him farewell and go back where they came from. But he soon saw that they had no such idea.

The eldest of all, whom Dickie knew as Cousin Dan'l, said to him presently:

"Cheer up! We know you'd be sorry not to have us with you during the winter. So we'll take a look at your chamber. Perhaps it's big enough for all of us."

Dickie tried to tell Cousin Dan'l Deer Mouse that he was afraid the chamber would be too crowded with so many in it. But when he opened his mouth the words, somehow, would not come. And at last he nodded his head and crept through his doorway, while his cousins followed him one by one.

The younger cousins pushed and crowded and quarreled, making such a commotion that Dickie Deer Mouse could hear them plainly, though he was some distance ahead of them.

"Those youngsters will have to keep still," he said over his shoulder to the cousin that was nearest him.

Everybody passed the message down the line. And when the youngsters heard it they began to laugh.

"Tell Cousin Dickie to stop us if he can," they shouted.

Their rude answer reached Dickie Deer Mouse just as he came to a place in his front hall to which he had paid little heed before. Right at the spot where he stood the tunnel divided itself into two passages. Before, he had taken the one on the right. But now something told him to go the other way. So he turned to the left, still followed closely by the cousin that was behind him.

The whole procession came trailing after them. And the first thing Dickie — or anybody else — knew, they all found themselves standing in the grassy pasture once more, in the gray light of the morning.

They had passed out through the back door of the house, without entering the chamber at all!

As soon as Dickie's relations saw where they were they looked at one another in a puzzled fashion.

"What's the matter?" Cousin Dan'l demanded of Dickie. "I followed the crowd. But I saw no chamber anywhere."

Dickie Deer Mouse didn't know exactly what to say. So he merely shook his head, hoping that the company would go away.

"Can it be possible that you've lost your bedroom?" Cousin Dan'l Deer Mouse asked him. "Is it so small that you could have overlooked it?"

"The bedroom's none too big," Dickie replied.

"Then maybe we passed through it without noticing it," his elderly cousin observed.

"We can't stand around here in the pasture all day, Dan'l," the cousin's wife complained. "If Mr. Hawk happened to come this way he'd be sure to see us."

"What do you suggest?" Cousin Dan'l asked Dickie Deer Mouse. "You see the women are nervous." And he cocked an eye up at the sky, as if he did not feel any too safe himself when he thought of Mr. Hawk.

"It seems to me," Dickie told him, "that we'd all of us better go back to our summer homes."

And then, after saying that he hoped everybody would get home without an accident, and wouldn't meet Mr. Hawk, Dickie Deer Mouse turned towards the woods and hurried away.

His parting words did not make his numerous cousins feel any happier. And since they wanted to get out of sight as soon as they could, they quickly followed Dickie's example and scurried off as fast as they could go, to spend another day in the summer houses in which they had been living.

Now, Dickie Deer Mouse had paused as soon as he had reached the rail fence at the edge of the woods. And unseen by his cousins he peeped back to find out what they might do.

When the three families scattered in three different directions Dickie Deer Mouse believed that he was well rid of them.

But by that time it had grown so light that he did not want to show himself in the pasture, not even long enough to scamper the short distance from the fence back to the front door of his new house.

So he passed another day in the last year's bird's nest.

XX

BEDFELLOWS

DURING his rambles on the following night Dickie Deer Mouse took great care to keep out of sight of the three families of cousins that had tried to quarter themselves in his new house in the pasture. Moreover he said nothing to anybody about his future home. Fatty Coon had taught him in one lesson that it is sometimes wise to keep a secret.

The night was not ended when Dickie sought the burrow in the pasture once more. He hardly dared hope, as he neared the dooryard, that he would not find a crowd waiting there again. But when he reached his doorway he saw not a soul anywhere around.

He felt happy beyond words. And he popped through his doorway, hurried through the hall—which was a hundred times as long as Fatty Coon's tail—and burst into the cozy chamber.

Dickie had hardly entered the room when he stumbled over something soft. And a voice that sounded exactly like Cousin Dan'l's called out in rather a peevish tone that he'd better look out where he stepped.

"Who's here?" Dickie asked in a faint whisper.

"We are!" the voice replied. "There are eighteen of us in all. And you'd better be careful not to trample on anybody."

Dickie's heart sank. He understood, in a flash, what had happened. The three families of cousins were all there, sleeping in his soft bed of dried grasses! They had come back to the house in the pasture ahead of him, and had found the chamber without his help.

At first he almost turned around and left that place forever, without saying another word. But the night had turned cold and a drizzling rain was falling. And he knew that the roof of his summer home must be leaking badly. That underground chamber was delightfully dry and warm. And if

44

the twelve children didn't wake up and begin to cry he saw no reason why he shouldn't spend one night there, anyway.

So he felt his way carefully about the room. There was no denying that it was dreadfully crowded. But at last Dickie Deer Mouse found a vacant spot that was big enough to lie upon. And burrowing down into the bed of grasses he soon fell asleep.

When Dickie Deer Mouse awoke, after his first sleep in the underground chamber, he thought that summer had come. He hadn't felt so comfortable for weeks. And for a little time he lay quite still, half dozing, enjoying the delightful warmth.

And then all at once he came to his senses. He remembered that he was in the burrow where Mr. and Mrs. Woodchuck had lived, in Farmer Green's pasture. And he recalled unpleasantly the misfortune that had happened: he had been forced to share his snug bedroom with eighteen of his distant cousins.

They were still sleeping soundly all around him. And Dickie Deer Mouse made a strange wish.

"They're here," he said to himself. "And I don't know of any way to get rid of them. I only wish they wouldn't wake up till spring."

XXI

ONE WAY TO KEEP WARM

AFTER making his strange wish about his eighteen cousins—that they would sleep straight through the winter—Dickie Deer Mouse crawled out of bed. The sleepers filled the chamber so full that Dickie had to step into the hall before he could stretch himself.

For some reason he seemed to feel unusually stretchy. Generally when he waked up he sprang up at once and dashed out of his house, to find something to eat. But now he had half a mind to go back to bed again.

He did not do that, however, because he wanted to get away from his unwelcome guests for a time. So he crept through his long hall and crawled out through his front door, into the world above.

To Dickie's great surprise a startling change had come over the pasture. The weather had cleared while he slept and the stars twinkled in the heavens above him. And the hillside pasture was white with a thick blanket of snow.

It was cold, too—much colder than it had been when Dickie went to sleep.

Luckily a crust had formed upon the snow—a crust that was just strong enough to support Dickie's weight. And he made swiftly for the spruce woods, to hunt for his supper, for he knew he could find nothing on the ground, covered as it was by the snow.

Dickie felt even hungrier than he usually did when starting out of an evening to look for something to eat. But that was not strange, for without knowing it, he had slept several days and nights in the snug chamber with his cousins.

Dickie did not stay out all night long. Yet he took time, before he went home, to hide a small store of spruce seeds in a hollow rail of the pasture fence. He knew that before the long winter came to an end he would find that food in the woods would grow alarmingly scarce.

Long before daybreak Dickie Deer Mouse was glad to return to the underground chamber. And as he crept into the crowded room he thought it the coziest home he had ever had. He knew, at last, what made the place so warm. The soft, round bodies of his eighteen cousins heated it almost as well as if he had had a real stove.

It was lucky for him, after all, that Fatty Coon had told them about Dickie's new house. And now Dickie only hoped that none of them would leave before spring.

That snowstorm proved to be only the first warning of winter. In a few days the weather grew quite warm again. And to Dickie's dismay the three families of cousins waked up and went out of doors to get the air, and gather seeds and such thin-shelled nuts as they could find.

They did not eat all that they picked up. Like Dickie Deer Mouse, they stored some of the food in secret nooks and crannies, against a time of need.

That first early snowstorm had been a good thing for the dwellers in the underground chamber. It had warned them that winter was coming. And during the weeks that passed before the whole countryside became snow-bound they managed to gather enough nuts and seeds to last them through any ordinary winter — if they didn't eat too heartily.

When the real winter finally descended upon Pleasant Valley it found the Deer Mouse cousins quite ready for it. And even if Dickie's relations did wake up now and then, when the weather wasn't too cold, they slept soundly enough at other times, so that they did not disturb him greatly.

Even the children, who had pushed and crowded when they first entered the front hall of the house — even they were surprisingly quiet, when they were asleep.

XXII

QUEER MR. PINE FINCH

PERHAPS the winter was longer than usual; or perhaps Dickie Deer Mouse ate too freely of his hidden store of good things. At any rate, Dickie's hoard slowly grew smaller and smaller. And long before the day came when he bolted the last seed that remained in the hollow fence-rail he had begun to wonder where he should find more food.

While he had been sleeping the birds that stayed in Pleasant Valley during the winter had been feasting greedily upon the very kind of fare that Dickie Deer Mouse needed. Jasper Jay and his noisy cronies had taken good care that there shouldn't be a beechnut left. And when they had eaten the last sweet nut they turned to such dried berries as still clung to the withered stocks on which they had grown.

No longer could Dickie Deer Mouse spend so much time asleep in his cozy chamber. Instead, he had to wander far through the woods at night, thankful to pick up a bit here and there as best he might.

On those crisp, cold nights he had to scamper fast in order to keep warm. And often, when dawn came, he crept home still hungry.

At last Dickie's night runs lapped well over into the day. For his search for food became more and more disappointing. And afterward he often wondered what would have happened to him if he hadn't met Mr. Pine Finch early one morning.

Mr. Pine Finch was an odd fellow. He had a peculiar way of talking as if he spoke through his nose. Though Dickie Deer Mouse had seen him before, he had paid scant attention to Mr. Pine Finch. But when he caught sight of him on a certain chilly morning there were so few birds stirring that Dickie stopped short and watched Mr. Pine Finch, who was so busy in a tree-top that he didn't know anybody else was near him.

He was talking to himself. And as nearly as Dickie Deer Mouse could tell, he was remarking—through his nose—that he was having a good breakfast.

That news made Dickie Deer Mouse prick up his big ears. A good breakfast was something that he had not enjoyed for a long, long time.

At first Dickie couldn't quite see what Mr. Pine Finch was about. It was he, beyond a doubt. There could be no more mistaking his odd voice than his plump, black-streaked back, with its splashes of yellow at the base of his tail, and his yellow-edged wings. Dickie had a good view of Mr. Pine-Finch's back, because its owner hung upside down from the tips of the branches of the tree where Dickie spied him.

To Dickie Deer Mouse the sight, at first, was somewhat of a puzzle. He stood quite still, gazing upward in wonder. And then all at once he discovered what Mr. Pine Finch was doing. Something struck Dickie Deer Mouse lightly on his back—something that made him jump.

He looked all around to see what had hit him. And there, on the snow beside him, lay a bud off the tree above him.

Then Dickie Deer Mouse understood what Mr. Pine Finch was about. He was eating the buds that clung to the tips of the branches.

Dickie Deer Mouse quickly ate that bud; and then he waited, watching eagerly every move that Mr. Pine Finch made.

XXIII

A FEAST AT LAST

To Dickie Deer Mouse, waiting impatiently for Mr. Pine Finch to drop another bud out of the tree-top, it began to seem as if his good luck were short lived. Could it be possible that Mr. Pine Finch was so careful that he lost a bud only once in a long time—perhaps only once a year?

But as Dickie Deer Mouse wondered, a small shower of buds came rattling down upon the snow-crust. And Dickie Deer Mouse snatched them up, every one, and ate them hungrily.

In a little while he felt so much better that he called out to Mr. Pine Finch:

"Shake a lot of 'em down—there's a good fellow!"

Mr. Pine Finch fluttered to a perch on a limb and looked down in great surprise.

"Did you speak?" he inquired.

"Yes!" Dickie Deer Mouse piped up. "You know, I can climb a tree; but I can't crawl out to the tips of the branches, because I'm too heavy. So you'll oblige me if you'll drop a few dozen more of those buds."

The request surprised Mr. Pine Finch. His face told that much.

"Buds!" he exclaimed. "Why do you want buds?"

"I eat them—when I can get them," Dickie Deer Mouse informed him.

The streaked gentleman in the tree looked quite blank.

"What a strange thing to do!" he cried through his nose—or so it seemed.

"Strange!" Dickie Deer Mouse echoed. "Why, you've just been eating some yourself!" And he couldn't help thinking that Mr. Pine Finch was even odder than he sounded.

"That's so," Mr. Pine Finch admitted. "In fact, I may say that I'm very, very fond of tree-buds. But I'm a bird. And of course everybody knows that you're a rodent."

"I'm hungry, anyway," Dickie Deer Mouse retorted. He didn't mind Mr. Finch's calling him names, if only he would drop some more buds.

"You're hungry, eh?" the odd gentleman in the tree replied. "That reminds me that I'm still hungry myself. So I can't stop to talk with you any longer just now."

Then he turned himself upside down, as he picked out a promising cluster of buds. And before he had finished his breakfast he had dropped so many buds that Dickie Deer Mouse called to him and thanked him for his kindness.

"What! Are you still there?" Mr. Pine Finch exclaimed, gazing down at Dickie as if he were greatly surprised to see him lingering beneath the tree. "I must go away now," Mr. Pine Finch added. "But I'll make this remark before I leave: If you have anything more to say to me, you can find me here almost any morning soon after daybreak." And then he flew off.

Dickie Deer Mouse told himself that he was in luck. By coming to that spot early every day he could pick up buds enough—dropped carelessly by Mr. Pine Finch—to feed himself until spring came and the snow melted and uncovered the ground, where he knew he could find food.

So he went home and slept as he had not slept for weeks. And the next morning, when he went back to the tree where he had found Mr. Pine Finch, his eighteen cousins followed him. For Dickie Deer Mouse told them of his good fortune and asked them to share it with him.

As for Mr. Pine Finch, he looked queerer than ever when he saw that Dickie had brought eighteen of his relations with him. However, he bade them all good morning. And he seemed to be even clumsier than he had been the day before. He dropped an enormous number of buds; so many, in fact, that Dickie Deer Mouse wondered how Mr. Pine Finch managed to get enough breakfast for himself.

Perhaps that odd gentleman knew what he was about. To tell the truth, he had noticed the day before that Dickie Deer Mouse looked thin and hungry. His coat, too, struck Mr. Pine Finch as being somewhat shabby. But he said nothing to show Dickie Deer Mouse that he knew there was anything wrong. And if he dropped tree-buds on purpose, he never let anyone know it.

Anyhow, Mr. Pine Finch did not fail to appear at that tree a single morning during the rest of the winter. Before spring came the Deer Mouse family had long since decided that he was the best friend they had in all Pleasant Valley. And they all agreed that his voice, although he did talk through his nose, was the pleasantest they had ever heard.

At last the breakfast parties beneath Mr. Pine Finch's favorite tree came to an end. The snow vanished. Warm weather made the underground chamber in Farmer Green's pasture seem crowded and stuffy. And Dickie Deer Mouse said farewell to his eighteen cousins, because he wanted to look for a pleasant place in which to spend the summer.

THE END